Hydrants

Alex Passmore

Hydrants
Publish through Hatchlings Publishing L.L.C

This is a work of fiction. Names, characters, places, and incidents are the product of the author's imagination or are used fictitiously. Any resemblance to actual persons, living or dead, events, or locales is entirely coincidental.

To Em and Abbs

HYDRANTS

I remember the cars. My best friend was the first to embark on the journey of wheels and freedom and she brought me along for the ride. Her Toyota looked like a spaceship with glowing neon gages and gadgets that held promises of our liberation. Sitting next to her in the passenger seat was the first time I had been in a car without my parents or an adult that my parents trusted.

It was a nostalgic time of late night fast food runs and blaring music heavy with bass and pulsing rhythm. No one prepared me for the undiluted anxiety that inundates as I climbed my first step into adulthood by ordering a burger at a drive - thru window for the first time. We were on our own under the traffic lights, moving alongside other drivers who had no choice but to consider us a part of it.

I remember the passengers; friends, siblings, boys. We drove to school, sports games, and movies, but our most visited destination was to nowhere and everywhere. Some nights we drove to golf courses abandoned at night. Vacant and easily hidden behind the hills, it was the perfect spot. We used to roll down the grassy artificial hills as the dirt connected to our clothes in the darkness. The thrill always withdrew once our eyes adjusted, but that first roll down was terrifying and something.

Other nights we sat parked in an empty lot playing Truth or Dare or Would You Rather. I never knew why they called it Chinese fire drill; but I participated in the exhilaration of un-buckling my seat belt, running around in the middle of traffic, just to jump back in the car while clasping my belt back on before the light flashed back to green. I barely had time to breathe. Our nights were consumed with preforming these bizarre yet bonding rituals. Making decisions that were only ours to make and creating memories that we were in charge of and responsible for.

It was one of those nights when we were aimlessly driving the late night streets. One of the passengers suggested we play "fire hydrant." The concept: if you see a fire hydrant pass by, you race to slap the top of the car. The last person to hit the roof has to remove an item of clothing. The adrenaline of even considering playing the game was enough to make the whole car start humming with hormones. My friend and I giggled and the guys were daring us and insisting that we didn't have the guts.

We pulled into a familiar neighborhood and began our search. Trees whipped past like an emerald sea and I remembered when I used to think it was the trees that were moving and not the car. I miss when I believed that the world turned for me.

When the first red hydrant flew by, my friend, the driver, lost. She turned up the radio and used it as her background music as she danced, seducing us while she slid off her ring. I envied her confidence. How did she know that they would like it? The guys jokingly booed her while they laughed. The game went on.

It felt dangerous and intoxicating when it was me, who lacked the speed, last to reach for the ceiling carpet of the car. Everyone's eyes were on me buzzing with anticipation to see what was underneath, even if I was stripping only a sock. I could see the driver's eyes in the rear view mirror, wide and enlivened, trying to pay attention to the road while also stealing glances of the back seat.

I never wanted to leave the car. In the car I was the authority. It was my choice to play, to look, and to linger. I told my back to bend. I made my hand reach out. I instructed my fingers to detangle the laces of my shoes. I pushed my lungs to breathe in and out slowly as I felt my face flush red from their curious eyes soaking me in. I delighted in the eyes and took my time deciding which piece to un-tuck, and even after I'd chosen, I did it slowly.

We laughed as each of us took turns stripping various clothing items of non-importance: buttons, earrings, and bracelets. I saw parts of my friends that I never knew existed. One uncovered a scar that looked like a vein in a marble slab, spreading throughout the skin then stopping unexpectedly, the trail abrupt and hidden by remaining seams. Another had a birthmark shaped like a triangle. I wondered how many others knew that about her or if I was the only one who noticed. No matter what life is like outside of the car, I know her. There were intentional blemishes too, an arrow that was tattooed on the skin by dipping a paper clip into ink and poking through the pores. Limbs of my body that were pale white, having never seen the sun, were now feeling the outside air blowing through the windows, for the first time uncensored. I felt as if my body was thankful for letting it breathe without the constricting fabric engulfing it. As if my body was aching to be with other bodies this whole time and be as it's meant. Skin that became insecure because I chose to conceal it, while other skin got to be free and change complexions.

We shed item after item, we could stretch and touch the wire as we were coming down to it. Someone soon would reveal a part of him or herself that would stir sensations of wanting and fire. The car steamed from the heat of the boys' pulsating blood. All passenger's eyes were peeled on the road, searching for reds and yellows in the black, preparing for it. The thought crossed my mind that maybe some of them wanted to be conquered, their loss purposeful. They were desperate to exhibit all of themselves for us. They wanted to be reacted to and seen.

My mind wandered with excitement as I imagined how far this could go. I thought about nudity and what it might feel like to see bare skin that wasn't attached to me in reachable distance. I wondered how my friends would behave; if they would stare or if they would laugh, or comment on the shape and size of it. I rehearsed and preformed my reaction in my head so I wouldn't make anyone feel uncomfortable. If someone undressed in front of me I would glance and quickly look away and observe the others reactions. I would be embarrassed for them to see my wanting. For them to suspect that my underwear was wet with expectation.

I wondered what could happen after. Would the stripper stay exposed? Would someone respond to his or her naked-ness by acting out human instinct? I was warm and aroused, surrendering to my own human motives.

Interrupted by laughs and playful whistles, I looked up as everyone's hand, other than mine, was raised in the air. My audience gaped as they waited for me to do my part.

I couldn't move. My bones disconnected from my brain. I begged them to move, but they no longer wanted to be a part of me. The bones in my arms had no desire to lift my elbows over my head and help maneuver the cloth up and across my chest. I asked them why? They didn't answer. My fingers folded into fists and my nails dug into the palms of my hands. I pleaded with them. All ten remained clenched in their position, hurting me. My eyes blurred. They refused to meet the other hazels that were gazed upon them. I yelled, please do something! My eyes could salvage this unbearable pause. They could let them know that it's okay and restore the lightness of the evening. My eyelids drooped and silently protested my demands by leaking out salt-water droplets that splashed off of my tightly grasped knuckles for all of them to see. The feelings that were so heavily felt a few minutes before dissipated and were replaced by static. The car swarmed with awkwardness, anger, and disappointment. The anticipation of it all was sucked up and circulated out through the air vents, my prude-ness a vacuum for their amusement. The steam that clouded the windows was replaced with clear and cold transparency. The foreplay was ruined.

The guys in the car became impatient. We approached a red light. "What the fuck is the point of this then?" said one and hopped out of the car with a slam of the door. The other two boys followed while mumbling their goodbyes. My friend wasn't mad at me, but I could tell that I had embarrassed her. She was mortified that she had such a prude of a passenger. I was no longer a part of it. I mimicked their body language and rhetoric but what I needed was a director to give me movement and action to match a social script.

He could say, "*Reach behind your back and unhook your bra. Smile shyly. Let them look at the soft pink of your nipples for just a second then cover yourself and laugh. Action!*"

No one was there to direct my insecurity, so instead the plot thickened with shame. The onlookers now know that I am a tease. My mind now knows that my body cannot be trusted. My own flesh ignored my urgent messages that were vibrating throughout my nervous system. They are on different sides now. My body no longer belonged to me. My mind was isolated, desperately trying to find its way back to control.

Now I subconsciously seek out the red and yellow statues, searching for redemption, but still they stare me down as I go by. It is as if I have signed an eternal agreement that makes me a lifelong participant in their game. The red ones are angry. They glare at me as I drive by because they know that I lack the courage to disrobe. They are wordless but their outraged stances are silently screaming at me, "What the fuck is the point of this then?" They go on with their lives but they look at me so I don't forget. How dare I?

The yellow ones laugh. I pass by them slowly to hear their jokes and they taunt me, still trying to get me to play. Sometimes I think that we are friends. They draw my eyes away from the roads but they wear sarcastic smiles. I dream about taking a hammer to its metal encasing and breaking the water free from their hold. I worry about the water trapped within their arms, absorbing their toxicity. I wonder if they tell the water what I have done.

The reds and yellows talk to each other when I'm not looking, but they speak in loud whispers expecting that I am listening. I avoid them. I take different roads. I turn up the volume and pretend to be somewhere they are not, but the hydrants are always there, creeping in the crevices of my memories.

Is it?

They take their seats. The screech from the chairs scraping the laminate floors engulfs the static air. She adjusts her sleeves and nurses the wrinkles crinkling her blouse. He coerces a noise as he clears the irritation from his throat. Before they begin, they identify the objective. The meeting will proceed as a performance review. They decide on a happening and agree to assess.

The old lovers had met at a bar, his friends there, too. It was late June and unbearably summer. Images of back patios and dripping condensation against golden sheens of beer glasses appear in both their minds.

Presently, they sit uncomfortably in durable chairs. Steam shines his face from the heat of the brown liquid in his cup beneath his chin. He sips his coffee; she fiddles with the paper that had wrapped her straw and she overthinks her posture. He reminds her that she called this meeting and should she start the dialogue?

Prepared, she flips open her notebook decorated with scribbles outstretching the lines and illegible handwriting ending with question marks:

What it is and could he tell her?

Whatever it was, it started as friendly. She was too young for rum and diets but the waitress didn't mind. Enjoying the shade and cool drinks they stayed awhile. The old lovers and the friends re-located to a small kitchen in a house to extend the good time. The neighborhood's uniformity and cut grass eased her in and she complimented the living room that was decorated with her mother's taste. The friends talked, but the friends were too witty for her to interject. She kept her lips pressed to her glass to give them an excuse for not saying anything. When she did talk, she said

"Yes, refill my cup."
"Yes, I love this song"
"Yes, let's dance."
"Yes, I like that, too."

Then there was the guest bedroom. She can see the scenes play on the screens of her closed eyelids like blotches, floating closer and then farther away. There was also a before. Saturn seats. Fields of grass. The longest drives. Longer calls. Letters from war. Movies outside. First times. She said yes for two years. Maybe she said yes in the after?

She isn't sure how to accuse.

He agrees there is discrepancy.

That being said, they get to work, ready to re-evaluate his business model. He pulls out his materials; a pointed pen and a fresh legal pad. He starts to bounce off ideas. He says that he himself is uncertain if it is. He points to her sober hinting. Could they write up a procedure for those circumstances?

She considers. Maybe if she weren't half asleep, her hip burning from the friction of the cheap sheets, it would have been more satisfactory.

They brainstorm ideas. They come to the conclusion that drugging her drink might have been an efficient tactic. Maybe she wouldn't have awoken and vomited all over the friend's bathroom floor. She could have slept undisturbed. The friends had been angry when she had dirtied the guest room sheets that had clothed her as she ripped off paper towels and cleaned up the mess coating the cold tile. He mentions the embarrassment he felt for himself, that his overnight guest had disgusted the friends. He had been frustrated when her vomit interrupted his cum. He had asked her for another fuck the next morning and she reminded him of the stomach acid stuck to her teeth.

He scribbles down,

1. Drug Her.

Moving down the line of topics, she asks, what about bruises? Suppose he could have held her firmly, stained her flesh so she had something to look down at. Her cunt hadn't hurt the next morning or even felt like anything. Could he have pounded her harder so that when she walked to her car she was obliged to waddle? They laugh when she shares her wishful dreams of him taking a crowbar to her temple and smashing it to blood and skull. If there had been something to show for it, then maybe they would know what it is.

Hesitantly, he jots down some notes next to

2. Force.

She proposes that he could have taken location into consideration. A bed is soft and welcoming, with not even a headboard to slam her head against. She might have felt differently if her back was stiff against a rough pavement in a back ally. Would it have a name if her shoulder blades had been jammed between small rocks and cigarette butts? The smell of smoke intertwined to her freshly dead ends could explain. Her sore back would have given a reason for sleeplessness. She would toss, turn, kick her legs out, cover them back up, and she would have something to write on the birth certificate. His mouth turns. She folds his hand around the plastic of his pen and writes for him,

3. Location.

As she used his hand, she could feel its lifeless, cold like the coffee had turned. Participation ends so she closes with a final thought. After the fact, she would prefer it if there were no communication. Then she would have known that she could call it a something. Then she would see it in the street and yell its name, calling it over to her. It would turn around and smile as it walked across the street to meet her. She would talk small with it for a little while. If it went well, she would invite it over for brunch. They would eat potatoes and eggs together and it would have one too many mimosas while telling her everything she wanted to know.

4. Ghost

Wrinkled Paper

My mother handed me a sheet of paper and instructed me to crumble it. I did as mother said and clutched the paper into a fist. I handed her the crinkled ball and she asked if I thought I could smooth it back out. How could she write with so many ridges?

I flattened the crevices and folds of the paper and pressed my fingers over the grooves and waves. When that didn't work, I strapped on some boots and stomped on it. I took it to the edge of the kitchen counter-top and slid it up and down the side of the marble. I placed the paper against the warm sidewalk concrete and rode over it with the tires of my bike. I laid it against the bathroom tiles and ran a hot shower, letting the paper soak in the steam.

I returned the sheet to mother, imperfect still, but she gave me a new leaf. Mother told me I couldn't take anything back.

I held the fresh sheet to my chest and Responsibility filled me up and drove me. It picked me up and dropped me off. It waited for me outside, patiently flipping through magazines in the driver's seat with its hazard lights flashing. She frequently looked over my shoulder, making sure my paper remained unsoiled.

On windy days I stayed indoors and kept my paper beneath my bed, tucked under a box of winter clothes. The wind wanted to sweep the paper out of my grasp and wisp it away. Responsibility wrapped me in a blanket to keep me warm and made me a cup of tea. We sat together comfortably, drinking in the warmth and talking strategy.

She reminded me of my posture by pushing my shoulders back and lifting my chin. She pulled down my skirt and crossed my legs for me. I stood still and straight like the paper she protected. I walked carefully through the hallways, never stopping to gossip or ask questions. I looked down at my feet moving forward to make sure of a clear path.

On stormy days, I'd wait for the rain to stop, crouching under coverings and not willing to risk drops sinking into my paper. Keeping my distance from the wet, I stopped washing my hair and it became heavy with oil. If I had to take a drink, I'd lift my cup steady to my lips and suck in small splash-less sips. I didn't swim in the summers or eat popsicles to cool off. I watched as other girls bathed in the sun with red juice dripping down their lips.

On sunny days, my eyes scrunched in the brightness, threatening to leave lines and dips in my skin. Responsibility held an umbrella over my head to shade me. Comedians came to see me to tell me their jokes. They had a competition, competing for who could make my face collapse with a smile or a laugh. My cheek's bones froze and never twitched. My soft flesh stayed in place without even a ripple. My stiffness scared the comedians away. They stopped trying and I became even more prudent.

I entered rooms with caution, sweeping the space through my peripherals looking for hazardous objects that could cause a dent. All the corners looked sharp and all the fingernails seemed long. I kept my hands to my side and took slow calculated strides, hoping that nothing would confront me. Dust swirled around me and thought about landing. Responsibility would wipe me down with a rag at the end of the day, brushing off any leftover dust that had made it onto my body. She slicked back my oily hair and pinned it out of the way and into a bun. When the specks of dust were gone, she took a steamer out of the coat closet and sprayed me down with warm smoke that melted my dirty thoughts away.

The day came when mother asked me for a paper to write on. I proudly presented to her a clean sheet; the white not even a little bit faded. Responsibility kissed me on the forehead and tucked me in to sleep. I pretended to dream until she left me. I spent my night wondering about what mother would create on the paper that I kept so pure. I imagined her pressing the ink into the page, the white soaking it up to make thick lines. Mother would be careful not to smudge the ink. She would write the letters meticulously to make the words flow. I dreamed of a beautiful poem, or a story, maybe a limerick for me to keep.

I woke up the next morning to find the sheet of paper lying in the open on the kitchen counter. A drop of water had splashed from the sink and made a transparent circle on the bottom corner. Mother had scrawled a list of items on it

Bananas
Paper towels
Shampoo
Tea bags
Crackers
Green Onions

CLUMSY

I tuck him in to bed and I watch him fall asleep. The glow of the TV lightens his face and then darkens it again as the show plays to keep me company. As the shadows play on his cheeks, he looks like different people. His chest rises big and his lungs suck in the air that swirls around us and releases it back to me. That's when I notice the dust and filth that floats around his mouth. I wonder if when he breathes in; does it float down his throat and collect until his chest fills up? I stay up too late online shopping for air purifiers. I take deeper breaths that night, trying to suck in as much of the particles as I can to spare his lungs.

Every morning he wakes up hungry. He goes into the kitchen and I lie in bed and listen to the sound of pots and pans clanging and the sink running. I fall back asleep and I wake up to silence, not sure how long it has been since I last heard him. I stop living so I can listen for any indication that he is still alive. I hope that he didn't burn his hand on a hot handle or leave the oven on. Did he leave the gas on and is he passed out on the kitchen tiles? I leap out of bed and run into the living room to find him watching the news and eating his breakfast. He smiles and makes me a plate. For a second, I was convinced that he never even existed. When he left for work, I took a toothbrush to the grout of the kitchen in case he ever decided to lie down on it.

On my drive to work I play back images of him twirling his hair and reading his phone. I envision a terrible accident. He had been driving, on his way to get coffee, and someone ran a red light. He was crushed. I keep my eyes on the road as I take my unused hand and feel for the hard of my phone in my purse. I call him indefinitely until he picks up. He was at work and am I okay?

I work a full day and I come home to him. He cooks me dinner and tells me all about the good parts of his day. I wonder about the people that he works with and if they are kind to him. What else interacts with him throughout his life away from me? I think about angry customers, careless drivers, heavy equipment, and potential accidents. I tell him he should be careful. He rolls his eyes, not understanding why. I wish that I could fit inside of him and be his eyes.

We eat our dinner and then ignore each other while we watch TV. We take a shower together. I want to scrub him down and wash away anything that touched him that wasn't me. Too many hands, dirty air, and bad thoughts access him when he leaves our safety. We have sex in the shower, but I don't enjoy it because I'm scared that he'll slip.

When we lie down for bed, he falls asleep fast again. While he sleeps, I trace his veins so paranoid and sure that one of them could be disconnected. I listen closely, unwarranted but worried; counting his breaths to make sure they're even. I cover his pores with my fingers because I don't want them to soak in the sooty air. He has all these layers of flesh that are holding together independent organs that I need to work and keep him. Him lives in his blood, organs, skeleton, and cells.

I wonder what his blood knows about me. Do they know that I am here with them every night with only a thin shell of skin keeping us apart? Are they keeping me in mind as they circulate throughout his body? When he bleeds and they see me for the first time, are they surprised? Did they imagine me taller? They might have pictured me with short hair and freckles and would be disappointed to find me differently. Do they race when I undress? Do they want to know about my blood?

The lungs stay up with me at night and I talk to them. I'm not sure if they hear me or if they even like my stories. Sometimes I can hear them, as they both work together pumping him with oxygen, they gossip about him and me. They love it when we fight. As he yells, they pack him with air to gust out his frustration. After we've made up and I've had a shower, he breathes in my hair. I wonder if they're breathing in my smell with him. Is it him or the lungs that are breathing me in so deeply?

His feet are thankful for me because I keep them warm, but I am grateful for the times they pressed the gas petal for hours at a time to bring him to me. If it weren't for his willing feet, I would have never seen him down on one knee. They stand all day, holding his weight, but it's worth it to come home to my feet and my hands. When his heels shed, and they can finally look out, they are comforted to see me.

He gets a haircut once a month. I miss the hair that is left on the floor to be swept up and thrown away in a foreign wastebasket. Only the lucky strands that fell against and hug his pillow remember me and stay loyal. When the new hair re-sprouts, it's like we're dating again for the first time. When he falls asleep, the hair and I whisper and play twenty questions. They fall in love with me when I answer them nonchalantly and I pretend like I'm non-committal. I fall in love with them when they are goofy, but strong, and their ends are still alive and shiny.

The hands know me best. They sleep between us every night. When my hair grows long, and my brush can't reach the back of my ends, they help me brush out the tangles. They help make me breakfast and they take the trash out when it's dark out and I'm too scared to go alone. One drapes over my shoulder as the other carries my books. They hold my breasts like they're his.

When I see all of his parts moving separately, I realize how momentous a body is with all of its molecules and arm hair. I hope that each part carries its weight and doesn't clock in late or work with mediocrity just living for the paycheck. I hope they take their job seriously.

How can I help them keep him? I want to stack cement blocks around him and seal him in. I think to put a cement roof over his head and add a small window so I can bring him snacks; but then I remember his legs. Would I care about his molecules and his arm hair if he couldn't trip over the hump of his calves throughout the day to make me laugh?

Surgery

$\frac{1}{2}$ brought a calm to Them. Maybe because of how she presented herself so evidently with childhood lessons of sharing and fairness that gave her away so quickly. As children, They noticed when someone else had more than Them did and them missed her when amounts weren't split even. They were taught that They deserved that balance. What a draining occupation to make the undeserving feel titled by solving all these injustices and disproportions. They and Them need her to be clear, to help draw lines and hand out ratios. Who gave them a warrant to take her a part and dwindle her down until this was their's and that was Them's? Her silence gave They Them the warrant.

They Them couldn't remain when she was mighty. 6/12. Her cadence claimed the top bunk and her kindness weighed down the bottom as a foundation. She made Them uneasy by being unmeasured with glances and not returning their inquisitive emails. They Them wanted to blink and say that she was.

The first step to determine her was to melt her underside that sat below her line and mold the leftovers. She was strapped to her chair and melded with a blowtorch until she was dough. They Them rolled her softness into a ball and kneaded her with their bony knuckles until They could build her back up to something They could work with.

They stuck her in a fridge to cool and then They used their fingers to slice through the chilled complexion of her stomach, as her 12 became a 6. To keep the congruency, Them discredited her ideas and spewed out comments about her immaturity until her confidence plummeted. The 6 slid to a 3 as blood and chopped flesh spread smearing the floor. 3/6.

She sat silently as her wounds were stitched closed. They Them rinsed her clean and rolled her into the middle of a crowd and swiveled her around for those to deduce. A mirror was held up for her to admire what They've done.

She hesitated to look; she could already feel what was gone. When her eyes met it, she didn't recognize it. Reconciling, she thought she might feel lighter in this new form. She told herself that once the slit healed, she would appear more assembled. She felt squeezed, but if she cut down on carbs she would be less contracted. Maybe someone could stretch her long. One could yank her arms while the other tugged her legs; the ones could pull her until she fit better. Someone could heat up an iron and lay her over a board. As the iron pressed her and smoothed her out, maybe it would make her skin stick to her new bones. She considered crawling into a dryer and spinning in the warmth until she felt refocused.

Placated by her settlements, she asked to be discharged, but They Them remained unconvinced. Still she seemed too sloppy and illegible for readability. To be able to compare her effortlessly, They Them would need to reconfigure her more. The numbers were punched and the blue prints were drawn up.

Without giving her time to recover, Them put her to sleep and dug under her already pierced skin. There were parts of her that were never considered. There was never a pro and con list of what to take and what to keep. Could any of her have been useful later? Nothing was recycled or placed in a bag for donation.

They sawed through her bone, back and forth until she was halved. Her remains were thrown into a bag labeled "Hazardous Waste" that would later be burned.

Them choked the 3's neck until she broke off into a 1. The 6 sat back horrified, waiting for the 1 to instinctively and sorrowfully shave her to a 2. She wanted to say something, but she didn't. Parts of her died thinking that they were defected and unusable. There was no chance for goodbyes. All of these pieces of her that had been connected for so long were suddenly missing and her remaining limbs sagged without enough support to hold her up. Why did Them need this from her? What did her transparency do for They?

When it was over, she dissolved into the classroom seat. They Them stared her down complacently, satisfied with her embarrassment. Whatever was left between her chest, sank to her feet and the ones all watched because now anyone could see everything.

Beside her, another student whispered, "Fuck I feel bad for you." The rest of the class couldn't meet her gaze, feeling the discomfort of her hurt feelings and inability to fit nicely. Relief flooded They Them as she was presented to the class as a half with blonde hair and big tits that never had anything intelligent to say after all.

Don't Take My Sunshine

I love the sun from where we stand.

She shapelessly fits into even the smallest cracks of concrete, bestowing life to the creeping blades of grass that poke out between the constricting grey and veiny slabs. She pulls all of it and us towards her. The trees reach out their branch, praising her and exhausting themselves to use up as much of her yellow as they're able. Warm water simmers and levitates up to her, brainlessly without a choice, as she sizzles their droplets to sky. Her light draws out the laziest alligators from the depths of murky lakes, to bathe by the grassy banks. They exert all their energy climbing out of the mud, just to have a small taste of her full exposure. Birds dive for fish and spread their wings wide to her, drying their feathers, taking the water, and leaving them sticky with salt debris. I walk outside and my skin exhales craving to soak up every ray until she is nothing, but she only stays for a short while, teasing us with her coming and goings. Taking what she wants. We need her and she only wants us.

When the night comes the lasting effects of her are palpable. The way I read sleepily in bed, still sun drunk with rosy pink cheekbones and lightened hair. Her after-shocks are evident in the way the trees look fuller with energy circulating through leaves and blowing softly in the dark. How everything is saturated with color even in the unlit. In the winters everyone dreams of her and fantasizes of how they'll be better when she comes back, and they'll get that thing done. The day that the sky opens-up and she brings us relief, we open ourselves to her and take her all in.

This summer, it had been a few days since my last dose of her. The weather, overcast and flat, had been keeping and hiding her bright fingers. Even when concealed I can still feel the heaviness of her humid. As I drove along the morning street I thought about her sleepily, the day would be better with her in it refueling me. Then I turned a corner and could see where there was a gap between the tall trees and the sunrise sky came into view. I barely recognized sun rising through the lifting fog. Hazy and orange, I could see the outline of her round, like a planet. The Florida smog covered her in a thin layer like a screen. I've never been able to directly face sun without squinted eyes and a hand hovering above my wrinkled forehead. As I experienced her so directly, I was startled. All this time I spent with her and it took me just a second to see it. In an instant, I realized that she didn't look like the infinite light that filled everything and unexplainably I felt wasted. My illusion of this reticent floating object in the sky that my bliss depended on so desperately, crumbled.

I couldn't tell you why I was so startled. I learned all about the stars, planets, and moon as a young student, but all those entities were so separate from my sphere. The world made enough sense and I didn't need a reason for it all to be. That moment, when I saw the sun for what it was, swallowed me up and my belief in the luminous completely deconstructed.

From here I loved her, but when I looked closer and she stared back, I saw how she floats alone in the dark silence burning the thick air, like a bonfire.

Thoughts of fire make me cold. Flimsy chairs in the dirt, wood burning, and visible breath. Once there is nothing left to burn, you're left in the cold with nothing to keep you warm and an overpowering smell stuck in your hair. You're tired, but you can't go straight to bed when you get home because you have to wash out the flame's perfume in the shower. You take off all your layers and let the hot water melt and soften the goose bumps on your legs; but the hot water doesn't have a long lifespan either.

I think they might have mistaken radiance for beauty, but only their fleetingness is shared. Maybe you can be beautiful and alone.

From here she is anything but lonely with the world below delighting in her offerings. She generously fills the oceans with vibrant colors and light refractions. She takes her time, slowly melting the ice cream on a child's cone for an ant to lick up the sweet drippings. Even though that ant would be quick to bite a child's flesh, given the chance. Weeds thrive and tangle as they emerge thanks to her rays. Some lands deplete. Acres of hot sand and mirages stand barren because she gives too much of herself.

What we wanted was to connect to a giver, but what is this life that she has prescribed? Outside of this, she is an island engulfed in a jet-black. Sun tells us it's okay to grow, but once we sprout so tall to reach her, we will be in the unknown too.

Icarus knows.

We are selfishly kept here because we are the company to her misery.

And we aren't the only ones she's fooling. Once someone tells the same story over and over, they begin to believe it too. She looks down at her reflection in the blue, gleaming back at herself, but she doesn't see her true backdrop, only the wooly clouds that she rests on.

I don't want to need her anymore. I don't want to see as she gets smaller and smaller, scorching herself to stardust. I tried to sit by the ocean and have a talk about all of this. I used to sit here and look up at her and think of peace and tranquility. Now, all I notice are her violent explosions collapsing her deeper into herself, all consuming. I want to ask her when will she have enough? Where's the line and are we any closer to it?

From here they sit and enjoy her, oblivious to her decay. She watches over us to keep her mind off of the pain.

Desperately wanting us to believe that she is all there is, but when she becomes a small burning pebble, we will all go with her and she will hand us our end.

I watch the water approach me and leave me, and back again. The waves glitter and shine to forge youthfulness and distract from our coming execution.

I don't want to live everyday wondering if today is the day that we vanish together.

Lizard in my Room

There's a dead lizard in my room. It's denigrating on my windowsill. I noticed it too late to watch from spoil's start.

It's body is caked dry and weightlessly paper already. Where did all of it's wet go?

For those days that I didn't know, I dreamt with death in my room, oblivious to a ghost that's been here for me. I can't help but wonder how it ended here in this way and if options were weighed before it happened. Did you think about ending it under the bed or in my shoe? Why not drown yourself in my bedside beer? I'd hate to think that you were confused and came here by mistake, or that you didn't decide at all.

I imagine an internal mulling over, view and comfort versus speed and solitude. I would want quickly and quietly, compared. It seems that you went out slowly, dying for an audience.

I check on it often, making sure to acknowledge it's lifeless whenever present. I don't want to miss a thing.

Now it's little body is cracking every where. A few days ago I noticed it's tiny fingers are on the doorstep of nothing. Only it's long sharp nails to show for a hand. I plucked a nail from the carcass and compared it to my own. Just a grey speck filling only a pixel of my thumb. I can only assume the terror those same nails brought to even smaller prey. To the moths and the mealworms, you were outsized. Is anyone else wondering about your thumbs?

Probably not and the responsibility to think of you weighs on me heavily.

Your eyes disappeared while I was at work. I dropped my keys on the entry and opened the door to my room not expecting change. I saw the two vacant holes staring at me. I don't know where they went. I swept the floor under the windowsill and sifted through collected dust and dog hair. I couldn't find them. Maybe this whole time they were withering and finally they shrank so small that my own eyes can't process the miniscule. I suspect that you're withdrawing yourself slowly so that it's not all at once. It's nice of you to think of me too sometimes.

When you couldn't see anymore, you and I listened to podcasts together. Never anything political. I played you *Crime Junkies* and we shared exasperation when the episodes remain unsolved. There are times when I need breaks from the expiring and I know you can hear me muffled from the other room, listening to the latest episode. Shame materializes out of something and come to find that you actually never cared if I ignored you because you wanted the space, too.

Dead things are the best at keeping secrets. When I didn't get out of bed for breakfast, you didn't call my mom and fill her in. When lunchtime past and I stayed put, your expression didn't imply my slack. After a missed dinner, when my husband came home, you didn't tell him about it either. The holes stared at me as I lied to him and said that I cleaned and exercised and showered. I'm not sure if he knows about you. Sometimes at night he rests the remote on the windowsill and I cringe, wanting to shout "Careful!" so that he won't squish you. But then he would know that I'm friends with the dead lizard in our room.

Eventually, your abandoned adapted into a final state of powdery grime. On the Saturdays following, I considered wiping you down with a wet cloth. Instead I left you, stuck in your dust form. I sprayed and swiped the night- stands and your filth remained a statue by the window.

Another day, when the weather was warmer, I switched on the ceiling fan. The blades slowly came to life, accelerating in circles. It rained down flecks of dust onto our white linens. The air swirled around the room and wiped you off the sill. Lying on the floor, outside of your curved silhouette, I couldn't tell the difference between you and the other remnants.

May 7th – moth in bathtub, wings separated but close by.

May 21st – 3 flies on bookshelf, but separate shelves. Friends? Possibly knew one another.

May 23rd – ants in guest bathroom shower. Possibly came up through drain.

June 18th – centipede stuck in tile grout.

9/15/16

I wrote you this poem from where things are better.

You inched me into a ship,
sent me spiraling out of a world that I hardly wanted to leave.

It took me months to break the solid atmosphere because
I kept going back.

Further away, the land glowed lush,

But once I stepped on the surface its ground turned dirt.

I learned to not look down.

Muddled from the shaking and heat of escaping,
I floated there for a while
Not sure what distant star to fly to.

I didn't know where I stood outside of hell.

That world gradually became a dot.

Effortlessly, I flattened it and you between my fingers.

Engraved in the swivels of my thumb skin, but out of sight.

I slipped past comets and debris,
All of it coming at me with bright speed.

It was beautiful compared to the nothing I realized that
you are.

A new world broke the darkness,
An easy landing.

Trees that climb further than the clouds.

The deepest oceans without the threat of sharks.

The only walls here are mountains.

To think I almost destroyed myself over a speck of dust.

•

JUDEAN DESERT

Sure, His answer was yes.

There was no prior interview process or trial run. He didn't ask to meet my family first or inquire about my history of heart disease. He didn't stalk my social media accounts or investigate how I was going to provide for us. There should have been obvious concerns regarding compatibility. We might not have enjoyed the same movies, or perhaps we had already signed opposing petitions pertaining to the fate of the oxford comma.

I need to buy cheese, apples, and crackers from the store. What if He needs to buy cheese, apples and crackers?

Out loud, it sounds like we want corresponding outcomes, but on paper it appears excluding, grouping two together to leave out the other. Is He that kind of person, or am I? Even worse, does He like pineapple on His pizza? Maybe He or I should have considered the longevity of such a request. I still had so much growing up to do, and he was past the point of evolving. A patient person would have taken the time to give it more thought, but I too had no questions or qualms about the whole ordeal. I'm not sure I even knew what I was asking. Either way, I asked.

After it happened, nothing happened. In the mirror stood the same person I've grown so used to observing every morning when I rinsed my face. After a once over of my appearance, I assumed that could only mean that this particular metamorphism was specifically internal and I needed some interior proof of the exchange. I brought out the scale from the closet hoping that the measurement would indicate an alteration of some kind. My weight typically fluctuated and when I stepped on the scale I was surprised to see the numbers reported on the lower end. Quite possibly this transfer or conjoining of spirits was ineffective.

Immediately, it registered that I could not tell my parents that whatever lives in them, had no interest in living in me.

Leading up to the event, I continued to beg Him compulsively and then run to the scale and check to see if I had gained Him. I thought that everyone in the audience would know or that the water would boil the bottoms of my feet as soon as my toes entered its holiness. My parents' only other choice would be to relinquish me into the fire.

When the day arrived, no one noticed He wasn't there. I didn't burn up and they clapped and cheered as my head submerged underwater. I got to pick where we ate afterwards.

"You're a woman now!"
"The Lord is in your heart!"
"We're so proud of you!"

I was the only one who knew that the celebration was redundant. The only soul that this body encased was my own broken one.

I forgot I had even asked until a night I had friends sleep over at my house. Like any normal pre-teen sleepover, we ate pizza and watched movies and when my parents went to bed we snuck on the computer to instant message boys. When the boys asked for pictures of our party, we took promiscuous snaps of our elbow fat squeezed together to make it look like we had rounded and voluptuous asses. We couldn't stop laughing at the "=]" that the boys sent back. The boy sleepover suggested that we join forces at the local park. My friends desperately wanted to sneak out and meet them and I did too. I had the perfect window to sneak out of. The top bunk of my bed met perfectly with the window in my bedroom and it was easy to quietly slip open the glass and jump through soundlessly. We set the plan in action and the girls all started to brush their hair and spritz body spray all over their prepubescent bodies. As the girls prepared for the convergence, I felt a stirring in the pit of my stomach. I knew what we were doing would be harmless, but I couldn't shake the uneasy twinge. One of the girls opened the window and was the first to climb through. She helped the others as they giggled and squealed. When it came to my turn, my leg wouldn't lift; it was made of lead. The insides of my body were filled to the brim with sand. I let them go as I stayed behind to miss out. When they were gone, I checked the scale and I realized I finally gained Him.

He saw everything through my eyes. I was so aware of his presence and I felt claustrophobic for Him. Without a choice, He went throughout my day without any comments or complaints, just weighing on me. I never told my friends He was there. I didn't want them to act any differently around me. I could feel His discomfort around the people that I chose to spend my time with. It was hard to hide Him. He never spoke. When we would go to church on Sundays, I felt lighter. I could feel His relief as we walked through the lobby greeting everyone and letting the elderly plant kisses on my forehead with their thin cracked lips. When I returned to school, the heaviness of Him hurt my shoulders. As if he spent the weekend binge eating.

I had to fight to do what I wanted. I used all my energy to move my arms and legs to move alongside my friends. When they asked me to go out, I struggled not to decline and stay in and read. I'd be stuck to my chair with a book; the only way to get up was to throw myself across the room. If I made it out, I was too tired from fighting the weight to build sentences and be social. I kept close to the kitchen and stood by the chips, keeping my mouth busy chewing. It felt like He was sitting on my shoulders, his legs straddled against my hips and his arms resting on my head. But it was me who asked.

At church I felt better. He unlatched from my hips and demounted my shoulders, letting me roam free. He let his guard down when we were with my family and dressed to pretend. Sundays always looked a little too bright outside. The kind of blue that looks ominous with white fluffy clouds promising Monday. The hue of a Sunday still repulses me.

Most of the kids in my youth group made me uncomfortable. I think because I could so easily be one of them. They live in a simulation where they feel excessively for some-one they actually know nothing about. They brag about how He talks to them all the time and they have their own secret language. He gives them feelings of comfort and direction, while all He does for me is add extra pounds, sulking on the tops of my blades.

I have one friend at Church and his name is Hayden. We first discovered that we were alike when we noticed each other keeping our eyes open during prayer. Now we play a game across the room of who can make the other laugh first. Not only that. Hayden asks good questions that the Sunday school teacher never knows how to answer. I love to watch her enter and scan the room and observe her posture collapse when she sees that Hayden is there and yes, he has already flipped the chair around in front of him so he can rest his feet up. She doesn't even try to hide her disdain. There are different colored sticky notes visibly sticking out of her bible where she's pre- marked bible verse to combat

Hayden's logic. I have a theory that they're color coded for the different genres of questions that he asks, but I'm not certain.

"Do you know that Jesus got mad and flipped tables?" Hayden asks, "Isn't that destruction of property? Like is that a WWJD moment or no?"

It's so weird to me that people fear questions. It's as if when you ask anything, then you are debunking everything they believe in. Although, Hayden isn't a good person. He can be cruel, and he doesn't inquire about interpretation and translation because he's genuinely interested. I do love to hear his ideas, though. I think he's doing everyone a service, wondering out loud about things that just don't make sense. I can tell it makes the other students in our Sunday school uncomfortable, but would they rather go off the deep end when they turn eighteen and find out the world is not what their parents taught them it was? Or slowly enter their awakening by learning to think critically. Critically or critical, which actually stems from the word crisis. Maybe we only ever learn when we're in crisis.

These are the thoughts that make me wonder if He would be better off in someone else. My salvation being a forever agreement just means that he is forever enslaved in a body that doesn't like the look of Sundays. Sometimes I get sick with the weight. My stomach feels so bloated with Him that I try and throw Him up.

I envy the people that never asked. Those who can walk and speak freely without feeling as if an anchor is tied around their ankles. My constant fear of disappointing Him is a prison that I requested and can't get out of. Once you know the truth, you're all out of excuses. But why is it that I know, and I still don't understand what it is I know?

Before church begins, I hang out with Hayden in the back and I watch him smoke pot. I watch as he carelessly puffs and blows, without any sign of distress in his body. I envy him for having no one to let down and I feel guilty for wanting no one. He asked why my jaw always looks so clenched. I tell him about the weight thing, and I ask if he's ever asked. He has. How are you so light then? I asked.

I think of myself as His Judean Desert, he says.

WHALE

Birds fly in the air, never having to return to the ground if they don't care to. They have endless sky to breathe in and belt out songs of anything. Worms scrunch slowly, digging in the ground or roaming above it. Ants are free to come and go as they please, entering and leaving their mounds. Seagulls plunge into the water just as easy as they fly out.

Whale saw the unjust imbalance encircling her. Exhausted by her diving, and her re-surfacing, having to choose between air and sea all of her life and never fully enjoying the potential of either world. There was never enough time to get to know herself because of the exhausting back and forth. She envied the fish that swim so deep, unconcerned with how much time they have left. Her body was worn from working unremitting and all she wanted to do was sleep. She felt halved.

Whale asked the universe if they could reconsider splitting her in two. The universe agreed, but she couldn't have both. She had to choose one: air or sea?

Whale made a list for each.

Air

- Sunsets
- Eliminating fear of land
- Could explore more
- Learn to waterski
- Take some classes at the college
- Write a book
- Discover new music
- Give weed a try
- Go to a concert
- Find and eat the best burger in the world
- Put an offer down on a condo
- Visit an aquarium
- Binge watch Netflix
- Meet a taxidermist and ask them why
- Get a blowout
- Get one of those vibrating fancy toothbrushes
- Learn the difference between 300 and 500 thread count
- Smell a campfire
- Watch porn
- Dive in a pile of leaves

Sea

- Family and friends live there – some of them are the worst. Opposing political views.
- Krill tastes good.
- I already know the best places to hangout
- I already know who my enemies are
- I have a standing appointment to kick Frank's ass
- I fit in
- Less change
- More romantic opportunities
- More beauty
- Less responsibilities
- Already in the upper class
- Explore my sexuality
- Make friends with Megaladolon
- Map the Bermuda triangle
- Laugh at dead pirates
- Swallow someone that stays alive in my mouth for a month and we become friends
- Go to Ocean-con and get an autograph from Triton

CUES

I think of them often.

I step aside in the grocery aisle. When we are stopped at the red light, I smile soft. I don't say, "fuck" out loud when they tell me the total. I put a t-shirt over my sports bra when I go running. When they ask me what's on my face, I say bug bites instead of pimples. I don't stare at the scar on your face, or your leg, or your arms. I write "thanks" at the end of all of my emails. I drive the speed limit and use my blinkers. When they tell a joke that's not funny, I laugh. I thank them for my ticket and tell them to have a good day. When I don't hear what they say, I nod. When they ask if I agree, I do. I don't ask why they don't have a job or why they broke up. I tell you about the weather. I tell you that there's too many books and I couldn't pick just one. I use my napkin instead of my hand. I assure you that it's all a part of a plan. I insist that it doesn't bother me and that I don't mind. I let them talk about their co-workers. I ask if they're a dog person or a cat person. When they ask to get together, I them that I already have plans or that there is a family emergency. I don't post the picture. I say, "Cute!" I don't wear the dress that squishes my tits. I wear heels even though I can't walk in them. I give them the aux cord. I let them pick the restaurant. I let them hold the door open for me. I don't lift weights in the gym. I don't tell them that they're a bad driver. I don't tell them what I think about their choices. I tell them that I liked the dinner they cooked for me. I answer their calls. I wave when we are walking to our cars at the same time. I don't shave my head. I ask how they are and tell them that we should catch up. I like all their posts. I don't tan naked. I painted my garage blue instead of green. I planted pink flowers in my front yard. I wait for them to be done. When it's their birthday I wish them a happy one. When their grandmother dies, I say that I'll pray for them, but I don't. They can have the window seat. I let them go first in line. I don't tell them that I dreamed that they were dead. I make sure that I'm on time. When there is a pause, I fill it. I paint my walls beige, and I don't hang up the Miami Heat poster. I pet their cat when I'm allergic. When they honk at me, I raise my hand to apologize. I let the barista flirt with me. I am polite to them even though I know they want my husband. I pick off the pepperonis on the pizza because I didn't tell them that I wanted cheese. I don't tell them about my dead lizard. I hide the vase they gave me in my closet instead of throwing it away. I take my shoes off and put them by the front door. I let them borrow my pen. My feet are quiet as I tiptoe, so that I don't wake them. I invite them to the beach, when I want to be alone. I ask for more details. I say "sorry" when our hands go for the breadbasket at the same time. I ask how their mother is doing. I sit with my legs crossed. I wear underwear. I say I'm good when they ask. I raise my hand before speaking. I sit up straight. I don't go on my phone when they're talking. I look them in the eyes. I chuckle at the meme they show me on your phone. I don't honk my horn and I wait for them to notice. I chew gum after eating garlic. I leave my phone on loud. I re-park my car until they have enough space. I don't send my plate back. I bow my head during prayer. I trim my pubic hair. I don't say anything political. I keep my music turned down. I don't return the shirt that didn't fit. I clap when their set is over. If the waitress didn't hear me, I don't repeat myself. I eat with my mouth closed. I make sure my breathing isn't too loud. I show up to the party with a bottle of wine. I stay when I want to leave and when everyone else is gone, I help them clean up.

Everyday I hope that you're comfortable.

Still Born

When I found out that my dog was pregnant, I was certain that it was an omen as to what was coming for me. I had just had my first real kiss on the side of my childhood home during a game of manhunt.

"Haven't you ever kissed your pillow before?"

The kiss hadn't lasted more than a second before my panic interrupted it. I was ignorantly terrified that receiving a half kiss from my neighbor had somehow spit cum into my virgin body and impregnated me. Guilt ridden, I took my mother for a walk to confess.

We had two dogs, one male and one female. They fucked like they accidentally stuck together. It looked like he just fell inside her and they couldn't get out. They weren't even moving, just looking at us asking for help. They also looked like they hated doing it but the universal gods of reproduction were forcing them to fulfill their destiny. My very religious parents let them mate undisturbed and allowed my siblings and I to observe. My theory is that they didn't mind us watching because of how sickening it was. It's possible that this was their way to persuade our subconscious to abstain, which in many ways worked. There were consequences to Missy and Buddy's actions and the laws of nature came to collect. This was also an excellent teaching opportunity.

Missy had her liter while we were at school. We came home before my parents. We found Missy inside her cage with black blobs and goo surrounding them. Every time Buddy tried to peek inside the room where his puppies weighed, she growled and snarled like a dead boat engine being revived over and over again. She let us stay. She ate the substance that was all over her puppies and as she licked and nuzzled, the puppies cooed. She let them suckle on her nipples and she cleaned them up one by one. The reason I believe in the higher power is because she knew what to do without pamphlets or Lamaze class. Witnessing her act on instinct that was not taught caused me to obsess over mine. Whenever my heart sunk or I got chills, I stood still and listened, asking my body what to do next. When I had decisions to make, I went with the first answer that popped into my brain. I studied those close to me and made lists of their possible instincts. Things like, my mother drawing me an oatmeal bath when I had the chicken pox; or my sister pretending to be asleep when I whispered to my boyfriend on the phone at night. When my dad held my hand as we crossed the street. Or how my sister and I kept my brother's secrets.

I called my mom and told her to come home. The whole family was electrified. None of us have ever seen anything like this before. My parents let us stay up late. We all crowded in the closet to watch nature at work. It was beautiful to see Missy care for her young. She stared back at us, amused at our interest, as if she gives birth every day. My sister was the one who realized that one black blob was stiff and still. Missy let my mom investigate as she carefully placed her hands in the cage and felt for the unmoving puppy.

She picked it up and carried it out of the cage and dumped it into the trashcan.

From then on, I only saw Missy as a mother. I wondered if she remembered her own mother or her siblings from when she was younger before she came to us. I felt claustrophobic thinking about how trapped this animal is here with us. Forced into a home where her kind is the minority and she's unable to decide or wander.

How many instincts has she lost being surrounded by white walls and food that is hunted for her? I wondered if her pregnancy would be any different in the wild. If she would know to eat better and exercise or if she wouldn't notice what was happening to her at all. How many generations of training and domesticating did it take for these animals to not want to eat us?

I felt sick for this woman that was so strong to give birth to four lives alone in a coat closet. There's no time to mourn the loss of one, because she has three others to nurture. She'll stay strong for them, because they lost something, too. At night when the others are asleep, she'll let herself grieve quietly. When they get older, she'll tell them stories about how their older brother was the most special. She'll stay up all night thinking of a response to their inquiries of what happened. She settles on, heaven needed a new angel.

Did she know he was dead the whole time? Could she feel his cold while he floated inside her, or was she blindsided? I wonder if his womb mates knew and felt his lifeless, too. Maybe they covered him with their warm to protect their mother from knowing the truth.

Did the dead one know that his body stopped growing? Did the others comfort him while he drifted? Before he was sick they talked about all the things they would do together when they got out. Their mother told them stories of the outside world and tried to describe what the sun felt like. When he got sick, they kept talking about life outside the womb and pretended that he would be there, too. Could it be, that their instinct was to eat him, to absorb all the good nutrients and leave the runt with nothing? Was it their fault? Does mother blame them?

The runt could have feared the horrors of the outside world, listening to us through the walls of his mother's safety. Maybe my brother's screams and threats about leaving scared him. He stopped eating, not wanting to grow big enough to be pushed out. Maybe he decided when his mother sat with me while I vomited in the upstairs bathroom. He dreaded coming out to see and feel me. He didn't want the responsibility of consoling me and taking on my worry. While his mother lay on the couch in the living room, he heard the people on the news sharing the terrors of the war. The gunshots and the blasts made him flinch and panic. He heard my parents talking in hushed tones about money and how there wasn't enough. He heard my sister scream for his mother to come back when she escaped and swam into the lake with the alligators. He felt her run and jump into the lake and he too started screaming for her to return. He felt our relief when we gave his mother a bath afterwards and held her close.

Or maybe he didn't know any of those things. He was unable to hear through the barrier of his mother's fur and organs. He was only aware of the bodies he felt around him, not understanding that those bodies were like him. They didn't communicate with each other or dream about an afterlife. This would be his life for the end of time. Darkness, and warmth, alone with his thoughts of nothingness and swirling blobs. Unable to handle the loneliness, he took control of the matter. That would explain his mother's complacency when he left. Her inability to mourn because her son chose to leave her on his own. She could have tried to reason with him and convince him to wait just a little longer. He didn't believe that there was anything to wait for.

The puppies stayed with us for eight weeks. We begged my parents to keep just one, but they insisted that two dogs was already more than we could handle. Missy's body was weak for a couple of days. She didn't come out of her cage and she slept, only waking to feed her children. As she got stronger, she started to wander. As her children got stronger, they too started to wander, and their personalities began to show. Each one was so different. One was frisky and stupid. Another, smart and sneaky. The third, a mixture of the two. Who before them did they inherit their quirks and charms from?

They played together and stepped on the heels of their mother everywhere she went. Their father was not to go near them, or the mother would snarl and bite. Missy's hesitation of Buddy as a father of her children intrigued me. Somehow, she knew to be distrusting of him and that made me hate him, too. As a mother Missy became wise to me and knew secrets that only mothers could know.

It seemed as if the mother and the siblings forgot all about the stillborn. The children understood their routine quickly and began to expect their next appointments. In the mornings they would wake up, eat, and then go back to sleep. While we were at work and school they stayed in the cage. When it was time to come out, they ate, and played, and then slept again. None of them questioned, what for? They had the luxury of not knowing the anxiety of figuring it all out. Even with a dead brother, they didn't know trauma or anticipate it.

If any of our brothers died, our lives would derail. We would go down a different path than the one we were to go down with our brothers alive. We would stay in our rooms and not come out for dinner. We would smoke cigarettes and make friends who make bad decisions. We wouldn't be able to keep relationships because of our inability to open up and our deep-rooted feelings of abandonment. Our grades would plummet, and the college applications would sit at the bottoms of our closets. We would be arrested for DUIs and petty theft. We wouldn't realize that we weren't good people until we hit rock bottom and then we would go to therapy and our therapists would say that we did all those things because our brother died.

When the day came for the puppies to be adopted there was no suffering. One by one their new owners picked them up at the house and the mother didn't care to lick them goodbye. She didn't tell the new mother that one is clumsy and to keep an extra eye on him. She didn't tell the new father what kind of food they eat or what time they go to bed. She didn't ask for their addresses or phone numbers to keep in touch. The only agony of the loss came from us. I had become attached to the puppies and their sweet characters and it was painful for me to say goodbye. Missy hardly noticed that they weren't there anymore. A mother who was a mother for eight weeks, acted as if it never happened.

It reminded me of an episode of a crime show that I watched. The captor forced the victim to do unspeakable acts, like torture innocent people and clean up afterwards. Eventually she didn't have to be locked up in chains anymore because she did it willingly and she enjoyed it. When they were finally caught, she had no memory of what she had done. It was appalling and devastating.

I cried because I know that that is what we've done to a mother.

Is someone doing this to me?

9 780578 717296